GIRLS ROCK!
Contents

D0543377

Jules *Rosa*

Fan Plan

Jules and Rosa are sitting in the back seat of Jules's grandmother's car on a sunny Saturday morning. Jules's grandmother and her friend Ruby are taking the girls to the local museum.

Rosa "Did you see Video Bits this morning? Jemma Dazzle was on."

Jules "Yes, I just saw the end of it. She's so cool."

Rosa "Jemma's in our town for tonight's benefit concert at the arena."

Jules "I know. I'd love to see her but the show's sold out."

Rosa "It's on TV tonight though, so we can watch it at home."

Jules "I wonder where she stays when she's here."

Rosa "Mmm ... it might be near here. Wouldn't it be great if we saw her?"

The car passes a sign for the Egyptian exhibition at the museum.

Rosa "What's this exhibition we're going to?"

Jules "I told my Gran we're studying
Egypt. She thinks we should see
some mummies and learn about
all that stuff."

Rosa "Cool."

Jules "Ahhh, mummies are creepy."

Jules's grandmother parks the car,
and they all walk to the museum
entrance. Rosa watches the people
going inside.

Rosa "Jules, Jules, you'll never guess who I just saw?"

Jules "Who?"

Rosa "Jemma Dazzle!"

Jules "You didn't!"

Rosa "Yes, I'm sure it was her. No one else dresses like she does."

Jules "Jemma Dazzle here? I can't believe it!"

Rosa "Come on, let's try to find her. She's got to be here somewhere."

Jules "This is a pretty big place. She could be anywhere."

Just then, Jules's grandmother walks over with the tickets. She takes the girls inside the museum.

CHAPTER 2

You Call That Art?

Jules's grandmother suggests that they all meet in an hour at the museum café. Before leaving, she reminds the girls not to make any noise and not to run around.

Jules "OK, Gran."

Rosa "Quick Jules, I think Jemma just went past."

Jules "Where did she go?"

Rosa "Er … I'm not positive it was
her. But she had bright green hair
and lots of black around her eyes,
you know, just like Jemma."

Jules "Cool, let's find her. Perhaps
we can get her autograph."

The girls enter a room with a sign on the door that says "Modern Art".

Rosa "Wow! Look at that!"

She points to an enormous painting hanging on a white wall.

Jules "It looks like something I painted when I was six."

Rosa "I think it looks like somebody spat out their drink on the canvas."

Jules (laughing) "Yeah, chocolate milkshake and vanilla cola."

Rosa "Mixed with orange juice."

The girls laugh so loud that a museum guide tells them to "Shush".

Jules (whispering) "We're supposed to be quiet."

The girls pretend to look at the painting, trying not to laugh. The museum guide tells the group in the room that it is worth £500,000.

Rosa "£500,000? For that?"

Jules "I know how we could make loads of money. Spit our drinks out on some paper and sell it!"

The girls burst out laughing again.

Just then, a woman with bright green hair and lots of black around her eyes walks past the door. Rosa tugs on Jules's arm.

Rosa "I just saw Jemma go that way."

The girls head off, on the trail of Jemma Dazzle.

CHAPTER 3

Paris at Night

At the end of the corridor, Jules finds a room with a sign on the door saying "Paris at Night".

Jules "Perhaps Jemma went in here. Let's have a look."

The girls enter the room, which is very dark.

Rosa "They really need to change the light bulbs in here."

The girls move to one side as the tour group comes into the room. The guide explains that this room is dark because the pictures must be protected from bright light.

Jules (pointing) "Look at this painting."

Rosa "I dressed like that once for Halloween."

Jules "Look how the dancer's standing."

Rosa "Her legs are so close together, it's amazing she doesn't fall over."

Jules "Especially with her arm above her head like that. She looks more like the Statue of Liberty."

Rosa "Let me try that pose."

Rosa tries to get into the same position as the girl in the painting.

Rosa "There. I look just like her."
Jules "I don't think so. Your arms and legs aren't straight."

Rosa "They're straight enough."
Jules "Here, let me help."

Jules adjusts Rosa's legs and arms. As Rosa tries to straighten her legs and keep her arms in the right position, she loses her balance.

Rosa "Heeelp!"

Rosa falls over. The girls laugh
again as Jules helps Rosa up.

Jules "Uh-oh, there's that guide.
Let's get out of here."

The girls continue down the corridor
to the last room, where the sign on
the door says "Ancient Egypt".

Jules "This must be where the mummies are."

Rosa "I've never seen a real mummy."

Jules "Perhaps Jemma's in there. It would be so cool if we could actually talk to her. No one at school would believe it."

Jules follows Rosa into the room.

CHAPTER 4

Come to Mummy

The room is full of people but Jemma Dazzle is nowhere to be seen.

Rosa "What a shame. No Jemma. But look Jules, these wall paintings are just like the ones in our history book."

Jules "Weird. The men wore little white skirts."

Rosa "And they all have black around their eyes. Like Jemma."

Jules "Didn't they walk funny?"

Rosa "Yes. Like this."

Rosa begins to walk with one arm bent in front, palm down, and one arm behind, palm up. Rosa leads them to a glass case, where the girls stop and stare.

Rosa "Wow! A real live mummy."

Jules "You mean a real *dead* mummy."

Rosa "Do you know how they make mummies? After you die, they pull your brain out through your nose and wrap you in a bunch of rags."

Jules "Ugh, that's gross. This mummy's all tattered and dirty. Mummies look better in the movies. This one gives me the creeps."

Rosa walks slowly to the other side of the glass case.

Rosa "I think he's watching me."

Jules "Who? This mummy? News flash—he's dead."

Rosa "Are you sure? Mummies come back to life all the time."

Jules "No, they don't."

Rosa "I just walked away from him and his eyes followed me. Really."

Jules "His eyes are all covered up. Stop it, Rosa, you're scaring me."

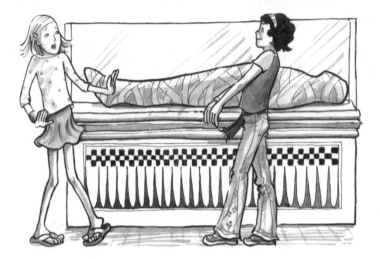

Rosa "How do you know he can't see? You don't know *what's* going on under those big bandages."

Jules edges towards the door. Rosa shuffles up to Jules with her arms out, doing her mummy walk.

Rosa (moaning) "I'm a muuuummy. I'm aliiive."

Jules "Stop it, Rosa. You're giving me the creeps."

Rosa (moaning) "I'm a muuuummy. I came baaaack to liiiife to get youuuu."

Jules steps backwards into the corridor and crashes into a woman with bright green hair and lots of black around her eyes. Jules is so startled, she screams.

Jules "Aaaghh! Aaaaghhh! Sorry ...
I ... I ... hey, you're not ..."

By the time Jules calms down, the
woman with green hair has gone.

Rosa "Are you OK, Jules? Did you
see her? It wasn't Jemma after all."

Jules "No, I know, but it really looked like her."

The girls see Jules's grandmother and Ruby walking towards them and they don't look happy.

Rosa "I have a feeling our museum visit is about to end."

CHAPTER 5

An Early Exit

Jules's grandmother decides it's time to leave the museum—before going to the café! The girls are really disappointed.

Rosa "Come on, Jules. I'm sorry for scaring you. I didn't mean to get you into trouble with your Gran."

With her eyes on the floor, Jules says nothing.

Rosa "I was only having a bit of fun. Mummies really are dead, you know."

The girls follow Jules's grandmother and Ruby along the corridor. Jules continues to ignore Rosa.

Rosa "I know we're leaving early because we made too much noise, but you have to admit it was fun playing Jemma Dazzle detectives."

Jules still says nothing. Rosa doesn't know what to say, so she shuffles along behind Jules.

Rosa (softly) "I'm a siiiilly muuuummy without a brrraiin. Someone sucked it out through my noooose. I'm sooorry I scaaared yoooou."

Jules smiles, then burts out laughing. The girls shuffle like mummies down the hall.

Jules "Tiiime to gooo!"

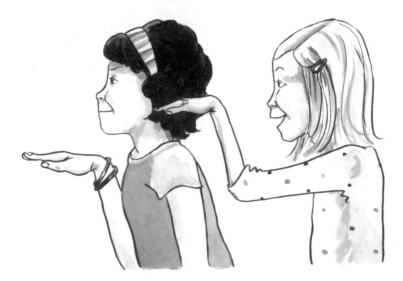

Rosa "Hey Jules, if it had really been Jemma Dazzle, what would you have done?"

Jules "I would have told her to watch out for the live mummy in the room!"

Rosa "I can't wait to see her on the TV tonight."

Jules "Me too. It'll be better than almost seeing her here!"

The girls walk like Egyptians all the way back to the car.

archaeologist A scientist who studies groups of people who lived in the past by looking at old bones and other old things.

artefact A useful thing made by someone, such as a tool or some art.

embalming A process used to stop a dead body from getting really gross.

linen What Egyptians used to wrap a mummy's body in.

mummy The body of a person (or an animal) that has been embalmed after death.

tomb A room or building where a dead person is laid to rest.

33

GIRLS ROCK!
Mummy Must-dos

☆ If you lived in ancient Egypt and you were an embalmer, you'd need to use special tools and equipment to preserve the dead bodies.

☆ If you're talking to a mummy, don't ask "Where's Daddy?". They've heard that joke a thousand times.

☆ Use a criss-cross pattern if you ever need to wrap a mummy with linen bandages.

☆ Mummies shouldn't hang around in the laundry or they might get thrown into the washing machine with the other dirty linen.

☆ You would need to allow about 70 days if you wanted to mummify a dead body. That's how long it took in ancient Egyptian times.

☆ Mummies shouldn't drive around in open-top cars because their linen bandages will flap in the wind and become loose. They might catch a cold!

☆ If you want to scare your friends on Halloween, dress up as a mummy.

GIRLS ROCK!
Mummy Instant Info

 Egyptians were master mummy makers, but mummies have been found all over the world, including China, South America and Greenland.

 To make a mummy, you have to dry out the dead body with sun, fire, smoke, or with chemicals. The Egyptians used a chemical called natron to dry out their bodies.

 Some bodies became mummies because of good natural conditions (such as extreme dry heat). Other bodies were preserved and buried.

 Some mummies are so well preserved that you can see what the person used to look like when they were alive.

◉ Robbers have stolen valuable jewels
   and things from Egyptian burial sites.

◉ Wealthy Egyptians had the fanciest
   funerals, which included hiring people
   to pretend they were sad by crying
   and throwing dirt on their hair.

◉ Pharaohs (ancient Egyptian kings)
   and other rich Egyptians were buried
   with lots of valuable things like gold
   and jewels.

◉ The only elaborate Egyptian tomb
   found intact (which means no one
   broke in and stole things) was King
   Tutankhamen's. He was a pharaoh
   when he was only a teenager.

Think Tank

1 How long did the Egyptians take to make a mummy?

2 What meant "king" in Egyptian?

3 What kind of cloth are mummies covered in?

4 What do you call a mummy's final resting place?

5 How did Egyptians pull the brain out of a dead person?

6 How can you preserve a body?

7 If you were hired to be sad at a wealthy Egyptian's funeral, what did you have to do?

8 Who was a teenage king in ancient Egypt?

Answers

1 It took the Egyptians 70 days to make a mummy.

2 "Pharaoh" meant "king" in Egyptian.

3 Mummies are covered in strips of linen.

4 A mummy's final resting place is called its tomb.

5 Egyptians pulled the brain out of a dead person through the nose, with a long hook.

6 You can preserve a body by drying it out, either naturally or with chemicals.

7 If you were hired to be sad at a wealthy Egyptian's funeral, you had to cry and throw dirt on your hair.

8 King Tutankhamen was a teenage king in ancient Egypt.

How did you score?

- If you got all 8 answers correct, think about studying archaeology. One day you could go to Egypt and look for real mummies!

- If you got 6 answers correct, write a musical play (that's a play with songs and music) about mummies and put it on for your Mum and Dad.

- If you got fewer than 4 answers correct, think about dressing up like a mummy next Halloween!

Hey Girls!

I love to read and hope you do, too. The first book I really loved was a book called "Mary Poppins". It was full of magic (way before Harry Potter) and it got me hooked on reading. I went to the library every Saturday and left with a pile of books so heavy I could hardly carry them!

Here are some ideas about how you can make "Mummy Mania" even more fun. At school, you and your friends can be actors and put on this story as a play. To bring the story to life, use some props such as a big poster with bright colours spilled on it for modern art, or a picture of a ballerina. Maybe you can wrap someone up in toilet paper to play the mummy lying on a table.

Who will be Jules? Who will be Rosa? Who will be the narrator? (That's the person who reads the parts between Jules or Rosa saying something.) Once you've decided on these details, you're ready to act out the story in front of the class. I bet everyone will clap when you are finished. Hey, a talent scout from a television channel might just be watching!

See if someone at home will read this story out loud with you. Reading at home is important and a lot of fun as well.

You know what my Dad used to tell me? "Readers are leaders!"

And remember, Girls Rock!

Holly talked to Shey, another *Girls Rock!* author.

Shey "Did you ever see a mummy at the museum when you were little?"

Holly "Yes, lots of times."

Shey "Really? Were you scared?"

Holly "Not at all."

Shey "Why not?"

Holly "It made me feel good inside."

Shey "If I saw a mummy, I think I'd be really scared."

Holly "No, you wouldn't. Not if you were with my mummy. She's lovely!"

GIRLS ROCK!

What a Laugh!

Q What's a mummy's favourite music?

A Wrap music.

GIRLS ROCK!

The Sleepover	Pool Pals	Bowling Buddies	Girl Pirates	Netball Showdown
School Play Stars	Diary Disaster	Horsing Around	Newspaper Scoop	Snowball Attack
Dog on the Loose	Escalator Escapade	Cooking Catastrophe	Talent Quest	Wild Ride

       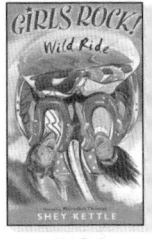  

Camping Chaos	Mummy Mania	Skater Chicks

GIRLS ROCK! books are available from most booksellers. For mail order information please call Rising Stars on 0870 40 20 40 8 or visit www.risingstars-uk.com

44